CHOICES

easy pass

By Eleanor Robins

Break All Rules
Broken Promise
Don't Get Caught
Double-Cross
Easy Pass
Friend or Foe?
No Exceptions
No Limits
Pay Back
Trust Me

ISBN-13: 978-1-61651-596-6
ISBN-10: 1-61651-596-1
eBook: 978-1-61247-242-3

Printed in the U.S.A.

20 19 18 17 16 5 6 7 8 9

Meet the Characters from

easy pass

Kaya:	has a hard time studying for history, Amber's best friend, worries a lot.
Amber:	Kaya's best friend.
Dax:	a student in Kaya's history class, cracks jokes in class.
Mrs. Holt:	Kaya's history teacher.

chapter 1

Kaya was at school. She was on her way to her history class. She had a test. And she was in a hurry to get to class. She wanted to get there early. She wanted to study for a few minutes before class started.

Amber was walking with her. Amber was her best friend.

Kaya said, "I wish I didn't have to go to history today."

Kaya liked to learn about things that happened a long time ago. So most of the time she liked her history class. But not on test days.

Amber said, “I know what you mean. I don’t like to go to science on test days.”

The two girls got to the door of Kaya’s class.

Amber said, “Good luck, Kaya. I hope you do well on your test.”

“Thanks, Amber,” Kaya said.

Amber went on down the hall. And Kaya went into her classroom.

Kaya went to her desk. She quickly sat down. Then she got her history notes out of her backpack. And she started to study her notes.

A boy came into the room. His name was Dax. He walked over to the desk next to Kaya. And he sat down.

Then he looked over at Kaya. He said, “It’s a little late for that.”

“A little late for what?” Kaya asked.

She didn't know why Dax said that.

"It's a little late to study for the test. I have tried that before. And it doesn't work. You need to study at home. And not right before the test starts," he said.

"I did study at home," Kaya said.

"Then why are you studying now?" Dax asked.

"Because I don't want to forget what I studied," Kaya said.

Kaya wanted to study some more. And she didn't want to talk to Dax. She wished he would stop talking to her.

"Maybe you should study more at home," Dax said.

But there was always so much to study for the test. And Kaya had a hard time studying all of it.

The bell rang to start class.

Mrs. Holt got up from her desk. Mrs. Holt was Kaya's history teacher.

Mrs. Holt quickly called the roll.

Then Mrs. Holt said, "You need to get started on your test. Put all of your notes and books away. Then get out a pen."

Kaya quickly put her notes away. And she got a pen.

Mrs. Holt passed out the tests. Then she said, "Time to start. Work hard. And no talking."

Kaya started to work on the test.

Kaya hadn't studied a lot of things that were on the test. And she knew she wouldn't do well on the test. But she still tried to do the best that she could.

The class time went by quickly for Kaya. And it didn't seem long until the end of class bell rang.

Kaya got up from her desk. And she took her test to Mrs. Holt. Then she went back to her desk.

Dax was at his desk. He looked at Kaya. Then he said, "How do you think you did on the test?"

"Okay," Kaya said.

But Kaya knew she didn't do well.

Kaya got her books. And she hurried out of the room.

Amber was in the hall outside of Kaya's classroom. She was waiting for Kaya.

Amber said, "How was your history test? Do you think you did okay on it?"

"No, I'm sure I'll get a bad grade on it," Kaya said.

"Maybe you just think you didn't do well. Maybe you'll get an okay grade," Amber said.

Kaya said, "I know I won't. I didn't know a lot of things on the test."

"Don't worry about it, Kaya. Or at least don't worry until you get your test back. Maybe you did better than you think you did," Amber said.

But Kaya knew she didn't do well. She didn't have any doubt it.

chapter 2

It was two days later. Kaya was at her locker. She had to get her history book. She had that class next.

Amber walked up to her.

Amber said, “Do you think you’ll get your test back today?”

“Mrs. Holt said we would,” Kaya said.

Amber said, “Good luck. I hope you did okay on it. And not bad like you think you did.”

The warning bell rang. And Kaya knew she had to get to class.

Amber said, "We have to get to class. I'll see you at lunch."

"Okay, see you at lunch," Kaya said.

Then Amber started to hurry down the hall.

Kaya quickly closed her locker. Then she hurried to her history class.

Kaya went into her classroom. And she walked quickly to her desk and sat down.

The bell rang to start class.

Mrs. Holt got up from her desk. And she called the roll.

Then she said, "Get out your books. We'll talk about the chapter you read for homework."

Kaya hoped Mrs. Holt didn't ask her any questions about the homework. She'd read the pages. But she couldn't remember all of what she had read.

Dax raised his hand.

Mrs. Holt said, "Do you have a question, Dax?"

"Will we get our tests back today?" he asked.

Mrs. Holt said, "Yes, Dax. I'll pass out your tests when we finish talking about your homework."

Then Mrs. Holt asked Dax a question about the homework.

Dax said, "We had too much to read. I didn't have time to read all of it. And I didn't read that part of the chapter."

"The answer is on the first page of the chapter," Mrs. Holt said.

"Oh, I guess that was one of the pages I didn't read," Dax said.

Some of the class laughed. But Kaya didn't laugh.

Mrs. Holt called on someone else to answer the question. Kaya didn't know the answer. So she was glad Mrs. Holt didn't call on her.

Dax looked over at Kaya. He said, "I hope you read all of the chapter." But he said it so only Kaya could hear him.

Then Mrs. Holt asked Kaya a question. And Kaya was glad she knew the answer to it.

Kaya was in a hurry to get her test back. So the class seemed very long to her. And she was glad when they stopped talking about the homework.

Then Mrs. Holt said, "I'll pass out your tests now. Most of you did well on the test. But some of you didn't."

Kaya was sure she was one of the students who didn't do well. She didn't have any doubt about it.

Mrs. Holt said, "Be sure you look at your grade. And at what you missed. And I want all of you to do that."

Mrs. Holt started to pass out the tests.

Dax got his test before Kaya got her test. He said, "Great, another bad grade. Just what I needed."

Mrs. Holt said, "Maybe you should study more, Dax. And listen more in class."

"Yeah, maybe I should," Dax said.

Some of the class laughed. But Kaya didn't laugh.

Mrs. Holt passed out some more of the tests. Then she gave Kaya her test.

Kaya looked at her grade. She was right. She didn't do well on the test.

Dax looked over at Kaya. "How did you do on the test?" he asked.

"Okay," Kaya said.

Kaya didn't want to lie to Dax. But she didn't want him to know she got a bad grade.

"Lucky you," Dax said.

Mrs. Holt passed out all of the tests.

Then she said, "Are there any questions?"

Kaya knew she had to pull her grade up. So she raised her hand.

Mrs. Holt said, "What is your question, Kaya?"

"When will we have another test?" Kaya asked.

Mrs. Holt said, "Next week. It'll be a hard test. So all of you will need to study a lot for it."

Dax said, "Not another test. We just had one. Do you have to give us another one so soon?"

"Yes, Dax. And you'll have many more before this school year is over. And you need to study for all of them," Mrs. Holt said.

Kaya knew she had to pull up her grade. So she needed to do well on the test.

But it was hard for Kaya to study for

the tests. There was always so much to study.

Kaya wished she didn't always have so much to study at one time. She wished just once she wouldn't have to study so many things. Maybe she could do better on the test then.

chapter 3

It was the same morning. Kaya hurried to the lunchroom. She wanted to see Amber. She wanted to tell Amber what she got on the test.

Kaya saw Amber in the hall outside of the lunchroom door. Amber was waiting for her.

Amber said, "I don't have to ask how you did on the test. I can tell by the look on your face. I'm sorry, Kaya. I hoped you did better than you thought you did."

"I got a very bad grade. And I have

to pull my grade up in that class," Kaya said.

"When do you have another test? Maybe you'll do better on it. And it will pull your grade up," Amber said.

"Mrs. Holt said we'll have another test next week," Kaya said. "She said it will be a hard test. And we need to study a lot for it."

Amber said, "I wish I had Mrs. Holt for history. Then I could help you study for her tests."

"I wish you had her too," Kaya said.

Last year Kaya and Amber were in the same class. And they could study for the tests together. And Kaya had done a lot better on her tests then. Most of the time, she got a good grade.

Dax walked up to them. He said, "Don't block the door, girls. Go in the lunchroom. Or get out of the way."

Kaya and Amber moved away from the door. Now Dax could get by them. Then they went into the lunchroom behind him.

The two girls quickly got their lunches. Then they went over to a table and sat down.

Amber looked around the lunchroom. Then she looked back at Kaya.

"Dax is looking at us," Amber said. "I think he likes you, Kaya."

"I don't think he does. He's so rude to me. Just like he was a few minutes ago in the hall," Kaya said.

"But we were blocking the door. Dax was right about that," Amber said.

Kaya said, "I know. But he didn't have to be so rude when he told us to move."

"But Dax is just like that," Amber said. "Sometimes I don't think he means to be rude. But he does sound that way."

The two girls ate for a few minutes. And they didn't talk.

Then Amber said, "How does Dax act in class?"

"Most of the time he's okay. He's always nice to Mrs. Holt. But sometimes he says things that make some of the class laugh. And a few times, he's been rude to me. Or at least I thought he was," Kaya said.

"I told you. That's just the way Dax is. I don't think he means to be rude. At least most of the time. And I still think Dax likes you," Amber said.

Kaya still didn't think he did. But maybe she was wrong about that.

chapter 4

It was the next day. Kaya had just gotten to school. She was walking quickly to the front door. She was in a hurry. She wanted to talk to Mrs. Holt before school started.

Amber called to her, "Wait, Kaya. And I'll walk with you."

Kaya stopped. And she turned around.

Amber hurried up to her.

"Where are you going? And why are you in such a hurry?" Amber asked.

"I want to talk to Mrs. Holt before school starts," Kaya said.

"Why? Is it about your test?" Amber asked.

"Yes, but not just about that. I'm worried I might not be able to pull my grade up. And I might get a failing grade on my report card," Kaya said.

"You worry too much, Kaya," Amber said.

"I know I do. But I can't help it. That's just the way I am," Kaya said.

And Kaya wished she wasn't like that.

"I can't talk anymore now, Amber. I need to talk to Mrs. Holt before school starts," Kaya said.

"Okay, Kaya. I'll see you later," Amber said.

Kaya went into the school. And she hurried down the hall. She got to Mrs.

Holt's classroom. And she went into the room.

Mrs. Holt was at her desk. She was looking at some papers on her desk.

Mrs. Holt looked up when Kaya came into the room. She looked surprised to see Kaya.

"Good morning, Kaya," said Mrs. Holt. "You're here early. Is something wrong?"

"I came early so I could talk to you. Do you have a few minutes to talk to me?" Kaya asked.

"Yes, Kaya. What do you want to talk to me about?" Mrs. Holt asked.

"I didn't do well on the test. And I'm worried about my grade," Kaya said.

"But that's only one test," Mrs. Holt said.

"I know. But I'm worried I might not be able to pull up my grade. And I might get a failing grade on my report card," Kaya said.

"Does anyone help you study for your tests?" Mrs. Holt asked.

"Sometimes my mom helps me. But sometimes she has to work. And she doesn't have time to help me," Kaya said.

"Can you study with a friend?" Mrs. Holt asked.

"I studied with my friend Amber last year. But we had the same teacher. Amber doesn't have you. So she can't help me this year," Kaya said.

"Don't worry, Kaya. Maybe we can think of something," Mrs. Holt said.

The bell rang.

School would start in a few minutes. And Kaya knew she had to get to her first class.

"Don't worry, Kaya," Mrs. Holt said again.

But Kaya would worry. She couldn't

help it. She always worried about things.

Mrs. Holt said, “I know you have to get to your first class. But we can talk about this later, Kaya.”

“Thanks, Mrs. Holt,” Kaya said.

Kaya hurried out of the classroom.

Kaya felt a little better now that she had talked to Mrs. Holt. But she didn’t feel a lot better.

chapter 5

It was the same morning. Kaya was at her locker. She had history next. And she needed to get her book.

Amber came over to her.

Amber said, "Did you talk to Mrs. Holt?"

"Yes," Kaya said. She got her book. Then she closed her locker.

Amber said, "What did Mrs. Holt say? Did she think you might get a failing grade on your report card?"

Kaya said, "Mrs. Holt said it was only

one test. And she asked me if anyone helped me to study for my tests."

"What did you tell her?" Amber asked.

Kaya said, "I told her my mom helps me sometimes. But that sometimes my mom has to work. And then Mrs. Holt asked if I could study with a friend."

"What did you tell her?" Amber asked.

"I told her I studied with you last year. But you don't have her for history. So you can't help me this year," Kaya said.

"What did Mrs. Holt say then?" Amber asked.

"She said maybe she and I could think of something. And she told me not to worry," Kaya said.

"I'm glad she told you not to worry. And I wish you wouldn't worry so much," Amber said.

"So do I," Kaya said.

But Kaya knew she would worry.

The warning bell rang.

Amber said, "We have to get to class, Kaya. I'll see you at lunch."

Amber hurried down the hall. And Kaya went to her classroom.

Kaya walked quickly to her desk and sat down.

The bell rang to start class.

Mrs. Holt called the roll.

Then Mrs. Holt said, "Some of you are worried about your last test grade."

Dax said, "You're right about that."

Mrs. Holt said, "I'll make a study sheet for your next test."

Kaya was glad to hear that.

"Will it have the questions that will be on the test?" Dax asked.

"No, Dax. It won't have what questions I'll ask on the test. But it will have a list of things you need to know. A long list," Mrs. Holt said.

Kaya thought they would have to know a lot of things. So she knew the test would still be hard for her.

Mrs. Holt said, "Also I'll have a review class after school. It will be the day before the test. And I'll help you study for the test."

"Who has to be here?" Dax asked.

"No one has to be here. It's only for those who think they need the extra help. And no one has to come," Mrs. Holt said.

"I'll try to be here," Dax said.

Mrs. Holt said, "But you need to know one thing. I'll help you to study for the test. But I won't tell you the questions on the test. So it will only be a class to help you study."

"When do we have to tell you if we'll be here? Do we have to tell you today?" Dax asked.

"No, Dax. You don't have to tell me at all. Just come that day if you want the help," Mrs. Holt said.

Mrs. Holt said she would try to think of something to help Kaya. And she did.

And Kaya would stay after school for the class. She wanted all the help she could get.

chapter 6

It was the next week. It was the day before the history test. Kaya was in her last class of the day. Amber was in the class too. Amber sat next to her. It was almost time for the class to start.

Kaya looked over at Amber. "I hope this class goes by quickly," she said." I'm in a hurry to get to Mrs. Holt's review class. So she can help me study for the test."

"Do you think many students will be there?" Amber asked.

"A few people told me they would be there. But you know how it is. They might come. Or they might change their minds and not come," Kaya said.

"What about Dax? Did he say he would be there?" Amber asked.

"He told Mrs. Holt he would try to be there. But he didn't say for sure that he would be. But he might be there. He said he got a bad grade on the test," Kaya said.

The bell rang. And the teacher started class.

The teacher gave them a lot to do. And the class time went by quickly for Kaya. So it didn't seem long until the end of school bell rang.

Kaya got up from her desk. Amber got up from her desk too.

Kaya looked over at Amber. She said, "I'll talk to you later, Amber. I need to hurry to Mrs. Holt's classroom now. I need all of the help I can get."

Amber said, "Learn a lot. And call me after you get home."

"Okay, I will. But I'll need to study. So I won't be able to talk long," Kaya said.

Kaya picked up her books and her backpack. And she hurried out of the room.

Kaya started to walk quickly down the hall. She saw Dax. He was talking to a girl in their history class. Her name was Marni.

Dax stopped talking to Marni. And he looked at Kaya.

"Don't walk so fast, Kaya," Dax said. "You might bump into someone. Where are you going?"

Kaya was surprised Dax wanted to know where she was going. He had never seemed to care where she went before.

Kaya said, “I’m on my way to Mrs. Holt’s class.”

“I thought that’s where you were going,” said Dax. “Tell Mrs. Holt I’ll be there.”

Marni said, “Are you really going to the review class, Dax?”

Dax looked at Marni. Then he said, “Yeah, I’m going to the review class.” But he didn’t sound like he wanted to go to the class.

“That surprises me,” Marni said. “I didn’t think you would go to the review class.”

“I have to go. I need the help,” Dax said.

Then Dax looked back at Kaya. He said, “Don’t forget to tell Mrs. Holt I’ll be there, Kaya. And don’t let her start the review without me.”

Kaya didn’t say anything. But she

wouldn't tell Mrs. Holt that. She wanted and needed all the help she could get. And she wouldn't tell Mrs. Holt to wait for Dax to come.

But Kaya didn't tell Dax that. She just kept walking down the hall.

chapter 7

Kaya got to Mrs. Holt's classroom. She hurried into the room. She was the first student to get there.

Mrs. Holt was working at her computer. She looked over at Kaya.

"Have a seat, Kaya," Mrs. Holt said. "I'm glad you could come today."

Kaya went over to a desk in the front row. And she sat down. Then she got her history book out of her backpack. She might have to take a lot of notes. So she got out a lot of paper and a pen.

Then Kaya put her backpack on the floor next to her desk.

Mrs. Holt said, "Some more students said they plan to come. I'll wait for them to get here before I start the review. And I'll keep typing the test until they come."

Mrs. Holt typed for a few minutes. Then she printed what she had typed.

Mrs. Holt walked over to the printer. She picked up the four pages she had printed. And she started to read them.

Mrs. Holt got a frown on her face. She looked over at Kaya.

"This is a lesson for you, Kaya. Always proofread what you write before you print it," said Mrs. Holt.

Mrs. Holt wadded up the four pages. She walked over to the trash can. And she put the four balls of paper in the trash can.

She went back to the computer. She typed for a few more minutes. She read over what she had just typed. Then she printed the test again.

She walked over to the printer. She picked up four pages. And she looked at them. She turned around. And she looked over at Kaya.

"I need to take this test to the copier," Mrs. Holt said. "The other students aren't here yet. So I'll take it now."

Mrs. Holt walked over to the computer. She closed the test document. Then she turned the screen off. And she looked at Kaya again.

Mrs. Holt said, "The other students should be here soon. Please tell them why I'm not here. And that I'll be back in a few minutes.

"I will, Mrs. Holt," Kaya said.

"We'll start the review as soon as I get back," Mrs. Holt said.

Then Mrs. Holt hurried out of the room.

Kaya needed to get a good grade on the test. And she knew it would be hard. And she knew it would be hard for her to study for it.

But there was one way the test wouldn't be hard. And that was if she had a copy of the test. Then she could study only what was on the test. And then it would be an easy test for her.

Kaya knew a copy of the test was in the trash can. She didn't stop to think about what she was about to do.

Kaya got up from her desk. She picked up her backpack. And she hurried to the trash. She got the four balls of paper out of the trash can. And she put them in her backpack.

Then Kaya almost ran back to her desk.

chapter 8

Kaya was almost back to her desk. Then Dax hurried into the room.

Dax said, "Did you just get here, Kaya? I thought you would've been here before now. I thought you were in a hurry to get here."

Kaya sat down at her desk. And she didn't answer Dax.

Dax looked around the room. He said, "Where's Mrs. Holt? Why isn't she here? I hurried here for no reason."

"Mrs. Holt will be back in a few minutes," Kaya said.

"She'd better be. I don't have all afternoon," Dax said.

Kaya was glad Dax didn't come sooner. Or he would've seen her take the papers out of the trash.

Dax sat down in the desk next to her. He said, "I guess you did bad on your test. Or you wouldn't be here."

Kaya didn't say anything.

Dax said, "Don't feel bad that you did. I did bad on the test too. We're both here for the review. So maybe we'll do okay on the test tomorrow."

Kaya still didn't say anything. But she should pass. She had a copy of the test.

Mrs. Holt hadn't come back yet. So Kaya had time to think about what she did.

Why did she take the test? She knew it was wrong to do that. So why did she do it? And why did she even think about doing it?

But Kaya knew that was the problem. She didn't really stop to think about what she was about to do. She just did it. And sometimes she did things without thinking about them. And they were things she shouldn't do.

Dax said, "What's wrong with you, Kaya? You aren't saying anything. And you don't look so good."

Mrs. Holt hurried into the room. And Kaya didn't have to answer Dax.

Six students came into the room. And then three more. And then four more.

Mrs. Holt said, "Find a seat quickly. And we'll get started."

"Will this take long?" Dax asked.

Mrs. Holt said, "I can stay for at least an hour. But all of you can leave whenever you want to leave. You don't have to stay that long. No one has to be here."

Dax said, "I want to be here. So I'm ready to start. I need to learn a lot."

Mrs. Holt said, "I hope all of you learn a lot, Dax. But all of you will still need to study some more at home tonight."

Mrs. Holt started the review. And Kaya tried to listen. But she couldn't keep her mind on the review. All she could think about was what she did.

Mrs. Holt said, "You haven't said anything, Kaya. Do you have any questions?"

"No, Mrs. Holt," Kaya said. She hadn't been able to listen. So she didn't know what to ask.

Mrs. Holt talked about some more things they needed to study.

Then Mrs. Holt said, "It's been over an hour. So time is up. Study some more tonight. And I'll see you tomorrow."

"Thank you for the review," Kaya said.

"Yeah. Thanks, Mrs. Holt," Dax said.

Some of the other students thanked Mrs. Holt too.

Kaya was glad the review was over. She couldn't keep her mind on it. So she didn't learn a lot.

Kaya hurried out of the room. Dax was behind her.

"Are you okay, Kaya?" Dax asked. You still don't look so good. I hope you aren't sick. So you can be here tomorrow for the test."

"I'm fine," Kaya said.

But that wasn't true. Kaya walked slowly down the hall.

Dax said, "See you in class tomorrow, Kaya." Then he hurried down the hall.

Kaya kept thinking about what she had done. And she felt worse and worse.

Kaya got to the front door. And she walked out of the school. She saw a trash can just outside of the front door. She went over to it.

Kaya opened her backpack. And she took out the copy of the test. Then she threw the four pieces of paper in the trash. She didn't look at the test before she threw it away.

Now Kaya didn't have a copy of the test to study. So she knew that meant it wouldn't be an easy test for her. But she would get the grade she earned. And not a grade she got because she cheated.

consider this...

1. How far would you go to get a good grade?
2. What would you do if you could see a copy of a test before taking it?
3. What does Kaya's decision tell you about her?
4. How do you study for a test?
5. Do you think Dax likes Kaya?